WAR ON THIS WOMAN, WELL TAKE THIS

ROBERT KLOWAS

LitPrime
"Your story is our priority"

LitPrime Solutions
21250 Hawthorne Blvd
Suite 500, Torrance, CA 90503
www.litprime.com
Phone: 1-800-981-9893

Published by LitPrime Solutions   07/27/2023

ISBN: 979-8-88703-227-6(sc)
ISBN: 979-8-88703-228-3(hc)
ISBN: 979-8-88703-229-0(e)

Library of Congress Control Number: 2023907123

CONTENTS

Dedication v

Chapter 1.   In The Beginning 1
Chapter 2.   The Adjustment. 5
Chapter 3.   The House. 8
Chapter 4.   Preparation Stage. 12
Chapter 5.   Midnight Requisition. .19
Chapter 6.   Solo Travel. 23
Chapter 7.   The Weaponry. 31
Chapter 8.   Get The Goods 34
Chapter 9.   Omar Abu Haggina Is Dead 36
Chapter 10. The Death Blow 40
Chapter 11. The Escape 42

DEDICATION

As children, my sister and I had a great childhood from our parents and grandparents. As we grew, we figured that when we had children, we would be well satisfied if we could make our children at least half as happy as us.

My Mother gave me the smarts, my Father the common sense; both taught respect and being an honorable person. I have tried to do that, more lately knowing that I have less days ahead than I have left behind.

That is why I stick with a New Year's resolution of being a better husband, a better father, and a better grandfather, for there is little time left for repairs. It is my regret that some repairs cannot overcome damages caused by others.

Thank You Sarah (Sadie) and Augustine (Gus).

CHAPTER ONE

IN THE BEGINNING

My sites are on the target; number one on the US hit list, chipping away, one at a time, and a gentle squeeze of the trigger will put him to rest. To think that I worked ten months for this opportunity, the boss wants it done, and now. With modern technology, this visual of mine is also being seen at the base and DOD and where else, I do not know or care. I have my job to do, and I really do it well. My Company is made up of 25 or so marines with specialized training to kill the enemy, and a technical support team of 10 men and women. Yet, I am the only female on the firing line, and leading the pack.

The image has been received by my boss. The red light on my scope went to yellow, the acknowledgement of receipt. So come on boss, give me the green light. What are you waiting on? The satellite will only be overhead for two more minutes, and then this connection is gone, along with Omar Abu Haggina.

The seconds tick away. Where is that damn green light? How many hoops to go through to get it done? And Omar Abu Haggina is about to leave his camp for where? Another ambush on our camp's patrol? Or the hospital again? Doctors and staff are so afraid to go outside for the terrific fear that has been put in on them.

I have been lying in this dirt for hours, it seems, but it's only been a dozen minutes. I knew exactly where OA is, good to great intelligence today. But the seconds still tick away and all I see is the yellow light, come on boss, get with the program.

The bureaucracy is fighting a politically correct war and it is getting me down. No time have I been so frustrated in my eleven years of work, then during this administration's micromanagement in knowing every detail of every operation. Let the good guys kill the enemy and break things. That was our training and is our mission.

Early last night, I crossed from Saudi Arabia into Yemen via the Oroug Bani M'aradh Wildlife Sanctuary some hundred miles north of the Yemen Border. Our Colonel has assigned two escorts for protection. Like I need bodyguards. They stayed in the safe zone south of the Sharorah Airport while I did my task in Yemen.

First, I need to skirt around a failed construction site of numerous single-level concrete buildings. Not knowing if any are occupied, scattered around a one mile area, stay clear, girl. A dusty nineteen mile trek southwesterly, I cross into Yemen. And 2 miles of ups and downs that these people call mountains, huh! Eight hours later, I am now outside the camp, getting into position some 700 yards away from my target area just as the sun rises, shortly after 0600.

Intelligence reported this man - that is wrong, he is no man, this man and woman and child butcher - is going to die today, any second now. So last night was in the lower fifty's, heat of this day gets to mid seventies, I can handle it, even with all my survival gear.

I am so obligated to wait for the go signal, under penalty of court martial, should I take him out on my own. Where is that damn green light? Only seconds left from above. Dame, NO, NO, a red light, it can't be, this is all so wrong. Damn, damn, those politicians did it again.

I am finished with this task and this outfit, screw you POTUS (President of the United States). Damn, now with all this effort, wasted, I must work my way back, northeast to outside of Sharorah to meet, huh, my body guards. Great. After nearly a day's walk and crawl back to the rendezvous point, something is wrong, very wrong. Where are the guards, only the four wheeler there? No contact because of radio silence we imposed earlier, too many ears out here. Got to walk around, check for snipers.

I have finished my 360 circle around a perimeter that I would be safe to spot any in ambush and there they are. Two sets of two are waiting for the kill. Well, last laugh on them. My slow crawling is a must, so quiet in this sand, but one twig snap, and I am with the dirt. One set down with a knife in each side, bye, and bye.

The next set got to be fast to get to, or they will know something is up when no signals are passed between them. Got to get it on now, quickly, 500 yards and two clean shots take them out. Effective range of this specially made German Sniper Rifle is 800 meters, so no sweat for those shots just now.

Onward, to the guards are where, and get out of here. Those damn bushwhackers' got my guys. No marine leaves a fallen behind. I place them in the 4 wheeler and head back to SA. Arrived at our outpost and I am still furious, more so that two friends of mine died protecting me and for what, another dry run, another drill, another false alarm.

This is the time, it was coming, to tell the boss off, but how far uphill can I piss at the politically correct crowd. Before I can say I quit this job at the end of my enlistment, the Colonel has some words for me, I am fired. Duh! The military just cannot fire an enlisted like that, can it? With two years to go.

The colonel expands; it is the whole damn company. Yes, the Colonel is a higher rank that a company CO usually is, but we are very unusual in our assignment, needing power at the top. So the Company is being disbanded and sent our separate ways when the job is not done. Where is the Cable Guy when he says Let's Get It Done; not in this Administration. All of us enlisted are being separated, WHAT!

We signed a "GAG" letter that we never will speak about our company and its mission, no mention of anything we did. A sentence of life in a not so plush hellhole if disobeyed. If you have your 22 years in, you are eligible for retirement at 50 percent of basic pay, and that is a big pay cut for someone looking for a 36 year stint. I, with eleven years get zip, zero, and nada. Oh, yes, a return flight to where I enlisted, not even where I want to go. This is surrender in so many ways. Thanks POUTUS.

I attach a hand written note to JJ and PK caskets for the families so they know exactly what they were doing, protecting me, when their lives were taken. So, So, Sorry.

That is another thing that irks me, their lives were taken; and they did not just give their lives for our country, as in the usual way of the statement. Maybe that all started with General George Patton quote:

"The object of war is not to die for your country, but to make the other guy die for his country".

At one time the US was the greatest nation with the military being unchallenged, now, still ranked close to first but we lost that distinction to China, Russia, India and the United Kingdom. Last POTUS reduced ALL the active duty to one and a half million, a loss of 700,000 from a half a decade ago, 2015. Now with a transfer of the support fleet and discharge of these marines, who knows where the bottom is. This action reminds me of the news clipping from 2013 DownTrend.com, which I keep on hand when the need arises:

"On October 12th, 2013, this story was even noticed by Dianne Sawyer of ABC News. You see, there have been 9 top level military leaders and commanders fired or relieved of duty since April. Is Obama preparing things for some sort of big event? There is even the strong potential for 16 US States being shut down and handed over to the federal government due to such high levels of debt. Could martial law be coming? There have also been reports that seem to indicate Obama has a litmus test for military officers these days. Apparently, he only wants officers who do not have trouble firing on US citizens. Several of these now retired officers have come forward and said that they think Obama is preparing for war against the US. We have also heard Obama himself talk about 'My Military.' Whatever you think might be happening, it is certainly clear that Obama is looking to change and move things in a different direction."

Yet we still have the war on terror, and no end in sight, not with that girl in the White House. I am so exhausted.

CHAPTER TWO

THE ADJUSTMENT

The Plan. I have no plan. Here I am back in the states without a home, car, or job. Am I glad to have saved every damn penny of my marine pay, less rec time expenses, so I can put myself into a *plan*. Those kills overseas were not without some treasure that went my way. Thank You. Each "victim" left me their id, I took a face picture, and all fingers printed, if they had most of their fingers. I am sitting pretty now.

All of a sudden, a plan comes together; I love it when that happens. I have the money, the knowledge, and the informational contacts that I made over the years, to take this to execution. I love the salt water, seeing a horizon, and fishing deep, like the Pennsylvania Lakes. What I need is waterfront, boathouse, and no neighbors within elbow reach. That should not be too hard to fill with all the shoreline of the Chesapeake and Potomac and their tributaries. Need to get the specs on my craft so I may have enough water for floating and avoid on lookers. So march onward.

First, a residence along the Potomac River downstream from D.C. is needed for several months. I can quietly gather the data where who is and when, and how to get there. The Potomac comes together along the Pennsylvania and Virginia state line, maybe 3000 feet above sea level. Then it flows east, downhill passing DC on the eastside and joining the Anacostia River on the other side of DC. As it passes DC, "ownership" of the waterway belongs to Maryland. Maryland authority crosses this waterway to the east coastline of Virginia for a good distance southward. How our forefathers decided on that, I do not know. Then the river continues toward seaward and joins the Chesapeake River before the Atlantic. That is about 380 miles, but I am only concerned with the waterway from the Atlantic to DC and return. How I remember these trivial facts from my Pennsylvania High School education along with the Expert Rifle Team experience is inconceivable to me. But I did do a lot of white water rafting and kayaking in the tributary at Cumberland, Maryland that leads eventually to the Potomac River, maybe that also helps me remember.

How does one rent a home using false information, ID, social security, credit background? Online, I must look for a Rent by Owner so fewer questions are asked, especially someone not wanting to report such rental income. I can and will locate the ideal property, but I must mask my IP address so as not to be tracked. That requires my first encounter for some outside help to disguise my inquiries while online. Sue can also set up my credit reports and a new personality. She is damn good and can use the money, again, thanks to POTUS, leaving her out in the wind, unemployed, last I heard. I get that done and I am on my way. Step by step.

A quick trip to Baltimore, near the Curtis Bay area, gets me to a friend of mine then to a friend in the Marine Company of Sue and where she is now. Has a job with the Chamber of Commerce for protecting their online system. Is that the fox watching the hen house? She is a slick talker. One thousand dollars for a new me, and several IDs if needed and a method to disguise the internet searches while online. Great. Another thousand to show me how to hook up a GPS to an auto pilot via a programmed laptop, thinking ahead for this mission.

Sue has her ears to the news more than I pay attention to national events; maybe it is her connection with the Chamber, but whatever. Being discussed at the White House is a measure to make military draft no longer administrative; it may be dissolved for eighteen year old men. Yes, we are a voluntary military, no draft needed as long as we get smart volunteers, not throwbacks from some court-ordered smartass judge "either signup or jail time", no need for those types. But no draft? What do we do when there is a national emergency or civilian pay is so good, military life becomes so undesirable? Well, then, why was I there, duh.

Then on the other side of her face is the theory that all men and women should serve two years in the military, the branch of service as determined by a military board if not volunteered. Their alternative to military service is four years in a voluntary mission, two years if outside the US of A. Their choice. An obligation that must be completed by age 30 and before college tuition assistance from the federal government is authorized. Our tax dollars at work. I see the end result of her two proposals is to blend and sell a new Office of Community Service. How does she go unchallenged?

CHAPTER THREE

THE HOUSE

Well, it did not take too long to get online once I followed Sue's instructions to the letter and number. Her process is much more secure for me than of the online ads for their security products. I do like the sound of the one "HIDEMYASS" by the title but let it pass for Sue's process. As I just stated, what I need is waterfront, boathouse, and no neighbors within elbow reach. Look at all the homes for rent and those for sale, not in the buying market, but those waterfront homes are so beautiful, how do they afford them and property taxes, yikes! Then, the list is gotten. To view them I will use my procured drones from one of my adventures, said I had recovered some treasures; besides the dead have no use for anything, anyway. Have any luck with those 77 virgins, guys?

Ok, so now for a vehicle to be my information and control center while I view prospective sites. Cannot use the same ID as in the motel; dig out another and a matching credit card. Off to my second contact, a minor auto rental company with little in-depth rental contracts. A Freightliner Sprinter 3500 cargo van will work so nicely for my requirements. This will provide a secure platform to launch my drone with plenty of room inside for me to operate my own CIC-Combat Information Center. There is an office in Rosemont, Maryland that is nearby. Well, I guess the military did me a favor by dumping my ass off in Baltimore where I first enlisted, now I am in close proximity to places of my needs and wants. But I will not stay here for long.

All of my prospective hideaways are south of DC, a nice ride on this fall day, getting out in nature. I will hit the closest one and work my way southeast until I run out of daylight, then return to each acceptable ones in the darkness to view these hideaways in a different light, ha, ha. The most important is the depth of water for access to the boat house from the main waterway, maybe fourteen feet depth, so as to be inconspicuous. At the boathouse, I need at least 8 to 10 feet at low water, preferable 14 feet; clearance to roof should not be a problem.

So I truck on down on the western shore of Maryland where most of the deep water of the Potomac is on that western shore; the main river tends to that side, not on the Virginia side. So interesting how nature created such a young river like this. First stop is in the area of Bryans Road. Potomac Heights is just off a 71 foot depth of water and this is where an owner has a 3 bedroom with boathouse. Excellent! So I get with him, find out the place is a duplex with a boathouse to share for each tenant.

This will not work; I need privacy to alter my vessel. Goodbye. Continue to the Village of Welcome, that is right, name is Welcome, Maryland. Must be friendly to all. There is a place off of Nanjemoy Creek worth looking into. A single family home, she says, with privacy, but the channel has silted in from the storms of this past winter, with no plans to dredge, I am at a loss here.

I did not do my home work on this. So, okay, onward to Piney Point. The description defies my imagination, for rent? There must be a gimmick? Bait and switch? "Grand waterfront estate with hundreds of feet of shoreline, some bullheaded on river. Boat ramp with boathouse over deep water, horse barn, private estate on 4 acres. Classic waterfront home of the period. Boat lift with remote control, gas grill. Whole house generator includes power to barn & boathouse, 500 gallon buried propane tank, fenced in with security alarms." From owner's ad on line.

As I make this drive along the shoreline, roads like Indian Head Highway, Chicamuxen Road, and obvious Piney Point Road, I make a point to pass law enforcement in townships and any county offices. There is something striking outside, an armored vehicle. I have heard of the townships acquiring a MRAP, or better known as a Mine Resistant Ambush Protected vehicle. Mine Resistant, isn't that an "overkill" for a small community? Paranoia of the government taking over this country is understandable. This will only intimidate citizens in a free country thinking that the police authority will not be able to be challenged legally. This could become problematic should the federal government, POTUS, want more power.

So I arrive and look and admire the scenery that I may be about to be a resident in. Yikes, massive yard, that is a good thing. This is perfect, so what is the gimmick?

There is a dredged area, deep enough for my access, with enough water to get to the main channel. I'll take it! The gimmick: The owner is being transferred overseas - Switzerland - with the company's assets, a federal tax benefit has been done away with. He will be selling this property on his return in six or seven months. AND. A new IRS rule has eliminated the Itemized Deductions, leaving only the Standard Deduction for all taxpayers, that is, those that pay taxes. So, no more mortgage interest deductions, his gift giving to the community and elsewhere, no longer can be listed; his income tax for next year is nearly his complete income, going broke in no time, flat. Since I have no income, I did not know about this item.

He tells me that this IRS rule will not be publicized until next quarter. The government's idea of not upsetting its citizens during the upcoming holiday season. The new reg does not become effective to the following year, the year prior to the general election.

This POTUS is term limited by the Twenty Second Amendment, so she has no problem, in her make believe world that the people will hear that the government will start to have a surplus, and will be able to help more people in need (making more people in need also). But that is only on the surface, someone has to pay for it. How the PEOPLE were bamboozled into voting for the Sixteenth Amendment, ratified in 1913, Federal Income Taxes over a hundred years ago, I will never understand. If those states and citizens could only see the fallout of what they did back then, they would be really, really, amazed.

And we walk the perimeter of the property; the front fence line of over 1700 feet has a remote controlled gate in the center, with his private road leading to his home, of two generations. I had a difficult time finding this entrance, passed it a couple of times, due to the heavy trees along the access road. Each side is about 400 feet deep, fenced in, and a beach with the boathouse out of sight of neighbors. How did I drop into this, what a piece of luck.

He continues on the history of the property, the inoperative lighthouse with museum that is downstream, and the longleaf yellow and loblolly pines his forefathers nourished. Not like I really care, but stayed polite for my ultimate goal. We made an agreement for a six month lease, where I take care of the entire property and pay him a modest $2,500.00 monthly. I paid him in cash, $5,000.00 for the first month rent plus 1 month for damage insurance protection. I see no problem, since I will leave it clean, and will not be back to collect. He will keep the deposit with no questions asked. So when can I move in, today, he can vacate now, his family is already settled in outside of Zurich. Well, all my stuff is in the vehicle, left nothing behind at the motel. I will call with my TracFone, tell them it is okay to charge me for the night, I shall destroy the key card. This made my day, get ready for the next item in the plan. The boathouse is well lit, a walkway on the three sides, with a remote control for the waterway door and the boat lift with a small runabout hung in the lift. The lift needs to be modified to keep the boat in place while lightly afloat, while holding my vessel in place underneath, covered by the water surface. Hidden.

Just some shackles and slings from a marina will do. I will give that stuff a new home tonight. I will let the drone scope out the marinas, and then make a quick in and out by this boat. Now for my next contact, the person that knows where the surface craft that I want, is moored and ready to be taken.

CHAPTER FOUR

PREPARATION STAGE

Havana, Havana, Cuba! What! So my contact informs me that the ideal craft that I need is moored with others of the same type at the modified and restricted navy base under the watchful eyes of the Castro's. Specifically, Raul Castro and now Miguel Mario Díaz-Canel. Well, damn, that will be a great challenge. These one and two-person craft are used to overtake and turn over any "escapees" from the Cuban Regime. Occasionally, these same craft dump over the refugees from Haiti trying to get to the Florida shores. Now, I want the ready boat, the one fuelled and ready to go.

Yugoslavia traded 3 or 4 craft for what, what does Cuba have of value to trade, irrelevant to my cause. It is very good that I was going to be sent to Miami by Uncle Sam and the most previous POTUS to plan an elimination of the Castro Brothers instead of waiting for their gentle passing. But the political action committee supplying POTUS with donations stopped giving. They saw that folks from Central America were getting priority assistance for entry into the US, and Cuba was left hanging in the wind, again. My recon back then was only the layout of Havana; I never got the go ahead to enter Cuba, or got to Miami. Then, the Great Appeaser makes a one eighty and tries to establish relations.

My idea is to creep in there at night, grab the boat, and haul up the Atlantic coast, but will this craft have that kind of endurance? A quick look at NOAA charts has Havana to Chesapeake Bay Bridge of about one thousand miles, a lonely journey for this gal, but will the craft get me home. Enough fuel for the trip? I have the time, for sure. This craft has on the surface top speed is 14 knots or about 15 and half miles per hour. Has a range of twelve hundred miles surfaced, YES! Beam 8 feet, draft three feet. Oh, it has 15 days of cell-powered system for below surface traveling, excellent. This trip will push my sub to its limits in order to get to the boat house from Havana. The Gulf Stream will give me a little kick from behind. This is quite a guess on my part. There are no torpedo tubes so other weaponry will need to be acquired.

There are a number of steps to take needed for a successful acquisition of this craft. Hey, it is not easy to get off of Piney Point by commercial means. A public landing strip a dozen miles up the coast may work. I may turn in the vehicle and grab a bus from Baltimore. No direct trip, I must off load myself along the route a couple of times with different ID's providing no trace of the same person. I really look good as a blonde or brunette or redhead, my ID's will match. From Baltimore I will go to Charlotte, to Savannah, to Orlando, to Tampa, then onto Fort Lauderdale. A lot of miles, more than 1300, and 3 days, but well worth keeping any hunting dogs off my trail. Forty minutes by the Tri-Rail service and I am in Miami.

Now the vehicle is back, and I am on the bus southbound as a brunette, Billy Jean. I will end up as a redhead out of place in Miami with all the blondes. I must get this done before the federal government imposes the ID regulation needed to go from state to state, some kind of heightened security for the safety of its citizens we are told. My Id's would not let me out of Maryland, but good for the time being.

There are four or five hotels near the waterfront that will make my surveillance easier and less noticeable. What I am looking for is a seaworthy boat with a low profile that can get me close offshore of Havana. One Hundred miles and plenty of Coast Guard and Cuban Militia to catch me. My one bag does not cause of concern for the desk clerk, a key card to the waterfront room, and just remember who I am this week.

There are a few marinas within walking distance, places to eat and sit, while I find the best boat. Watching for this low profile, just fuelled up, and the keys left for the taking, type boat, yes people leave their keys within easy reach, even in Miami.

While I wait for the afternoon and evening boating crowd to moor up, I scan the alphabet channels on national news, and who do I see, but POTUS on each channel. The main news media likes this POTUS and offers air time in hopes of keeping in good contact with her and her staff. So what is new? Oh, the country is in a security alert from threats overseas, nothing new about that. Omar Abu Haggina is on the loose, well, he always has been, but I had him in my sights sometime back.

Omar is staging an invasion of the US, oh, really. POTUS says we must be prepared. I was about to put his lights out when the red light came on, who you kidding. Was it you that put a stop to me and now you have American citizens alarmed; this, today could have been prevented, ok, that is it; POTUS needs a cause for us to rally around her. She knows no body messes with the U S of A in a crisis and she is drawing us into supporting her in time of need. What a bunch of crap.

During this time, I check in at the local scuba rental outfits to procure my gear. Rent or buy? Depends on the amount of questions, I have my scuba certification to match this redhead id. Truth is, I am very well proficient in underwater operations. Can't explain that to these outfits; just be amateurish, yet convincing. This one outfit has the up to date Nitrox system that will extend the dive time. A 16 and ½ pound sea scooter will be a great assistance once I go overboard from my craft outside Havana Harbor. An hour and a half dive time will be sufficient to get me through the entrance to the harbor. But where do I put this gear until I am ready and then get it unseen to the boat, starting to get complicated, and these logistics things. I always had people. Okay, a self-storage unit, climate controlled with 24 hour access; that will work. Eighty bucks for the month is good for me. One large trooper trunk with wheels will get the gear to the boat all at once, then get gone. People move stuff around in Miami all hours of the day and night, not much concern for being obvious.

Now for the hard work, with much patience, I must walk around the half dozen marinas watching for my victim. This boat with a low profile needs to be moored where I can get to the Atlantic directly and quickly. No intracoastal waterway, no canals. The main channel or Fishermans Channel will be the direct route, 4 miles to the ocean, so get out of my way boys, I am a coming. I walk, I sit, I eat, drink adult beverages a little, and observe. The city marina alone has over twelve hundred boat slips, and security. There are no cheap boats here, the marinas do a great business, dock space, fuel, and bait for the fishing guys.

What is it with the dock hands in light red shirts, dark blue pants, boat shoes, and WHITE gloves? Okay, so how many times do they change gloves, after every assistance to a boater mooring up? NAA. And they have a key box for storage of the individual boat keys? What nonsense, owners do not take their keys with them, or leave them under the seat, like I was planning on? The nerve.

So how about a plan girl, need a plan on the key box, keys, and matching boat. And with 24 hours security, damn. So I contemplate. There is no risk in renting a kayak, cash, and taking a break at this dock, just to straighten my back, of course. That will work. A quick taxi ride across Venetian Causeway to the Kayak Rental. So $40.00 for 4 hours, will then paddle the 3 miles across Biscayne Bay back to the City Marina, and make friends, ha, ha.

So, a taxi ride of about 4 miles, cost more than a 12 foot sit-on-top ocean kayak rental, wow. The dock master or rental guy wants me to know that the bay is safe for kayaking today, only a light chop, with 5 knots of wind. Okay by me. A quick compute, an hour travel each way plus or minus an hour, plenty of time for my trip. The State of Florida did an aerial survey determining more pleasure craft use the waterways on weekends than during the week. Well, how obvious is that. My intention is to disappear during a weekday night, or this Sunday night if I get the goods.

The 3 mile paddle over to Miami is a piece of cake, beautiful shoreline, birds, and manatees. I pull up to the City Marina dock where I can yell out to the dock hand about straightening my back for a few minutes. It just so happens, it is the main dock where the dock house and especially the key storage is. First, I notice the white gloves are covered with a larger plastic glove, that is how they stay so clean handling the mooring lines, wash off fast, back to work fast, huh. And I stretch my legs and body out for a minute, and then pursue my questions and answer period along with my minute camera mounted on my suit top, looking like an ornamental pendant. One part of my wireless remote triggering device is on my left index finger and the other is on the lower part of my suit, anywhere along the outside of the hemline, just a tap, snap it. Velcro is so good. The relatively easy discussion with the dock hand is not so easy; ya think he has a top secret clearance and protecting his stock as if it were his.

After a little coaching, I find out that single owners keep their keys with them, no requirement to turn them in to the dock staff. But there are two groups that are treated to a certain process where the keys are not for the operator to keep. First case, city owned boats that have qualified "renters" in a club, which by paying dues; insure that the boat is topped off with fuel, and left clean. They get charged for the rental, and the key is turned in to the dock guy. The red tags, numbered with the dock space number. Second, and more interesting, is the "timeshare" boaters that several investors have a financial interest in the boat, and contracted with all owners, the time period of use. They are also responsible to leave the boat in ship shape, but the dock hands have no need to inspect those boats. It is up to the owners to self- discipline. Blue tags, similarly numbered. In any case, these two groups are the ideal victims for my use, especially, the city owned with a good inspection upon mooring. My kind of boat, specific one still waits. Then there is the security and how to get that info out of him.

I'll take a walk, talk to the adjacent dock guy. He is not as tight lipped after my sweet hello, to find out that there is only one guard on duty during night hours. Sunday to Thursday, the 3 guards go to 1 at 10PM until 6AM. That is all I needed to know for now. Goodbye.

Back to the kayak after my goodbye to the first dock hand, and paddle back to the rental dock. Get a cab back to Miami, not stopping at my hotel, but elsewhere, and walk "home". Everyone wears bikinis on the streets here in Miami. Change clothes, get something to eat and watch the victims, uh, boats come in. This is Friday night; the harbor is very busy, just like the government survey said. Does the government include Fridays as the "weekend"? The three dock hands have about four hundred boats in their area, and my area of interest is where the night shift hangs out, has the keys; that key man is my key to out of here. I have tonight and Saturday to make a decision, got to go on Sunday.

I work this time line out on paper with the use of a couple of nautical charts. Starting backwards, got to get my mini sub underway during darkness. Sunrise for Havana is at 6:58AM and the earliest safe time to hit on the dock hand is at 10PM the night before, assuming the other two guards punch out on time. That leaves me nine hours to get underway, get to Havana, slither my way underwater to the boat, cause a distraction, and get the mini sub underway. Once outside the harbor or sooner, I dive and travel most of the day that way. Offshore sea conditions forecasted for Sunday night is 2 to 3 foot seas, isolated showers, water temp 76F. Doable with the right boat. Rent the twin tanks and sea scooter Sunday as well. I have all the other gear from my special ops days, wet suite, mask, fins, and especially the underwater GPS.

Yes, GPS does not work underwater by itself, but a transceiver on a Styrofoam float (GPS gateway) with a thin line tethered to my weight belt provides a signal to my wristband GPS. The transceiver has a range of up to one mile, since I will be underwater 4 miles or more, this float needs to be dragged along the surface, discreetly. Modern technology is so great.

But then, logistics not being my fine suit, I had people for that, they got me there, no fuss, no muss, I do the job, and they get me out. Now I must do the figuring myself. What is all this talk about Miami being 90 miles from Havana, non-sense? I am plotting the course on this chart; I get 240 miles from Miami Harbor entrance to Havana. I recheck my calculations, triple check, same results, and insanity. At

20 miles per hour, that is 12 hours running, not enough dark hours, shit. All this work last few days for nothing, zip.

So I must move to the Keys, Islamorada is 170 miles, Marathon 140 miles, Key West is 100 miles from Havana. Nuts! At 20 knots, that would be 5, 7, or 8 to 9 hours run time from those specific points just mentioned, respectively. Key West may be too illogical for a boat thief, like where do I go now that I am at the end of the world, sort of. Islamorada may be too far, no margin for error or regrouping if needed. So I guess I will head to Marathon. Now for my internet searches on marinas, hotels, and that specific boat. Cancel my orders for dive gear and storage, check out of this hotel. A one way rental car will get me there and a chance to look around.

Time a wasting. VPOTUS (Vice President of the United States) holds the annual picnic at her residence, the Navy Observatory, on time each spring. Not even the minority political party shutting down the federal government three years ago did not stop her party's fun. How does a minority party shut the government down anyway? Last non-presidential election, the voters decided they did not like the way this team was leading this country and voted in a majority of the opposing party in the House and the Senate. The "team" that was elected way back then was undefeatable, two wives from previous Presidents, each hating each other, but ran together for the greater good, their own egos.

CHAPTER FIVE

MIDNIGHT REQUISITION

The half dozen marinas offer a number of potential victims for my behalf. The weekend is almost gone, no thanks to my imperfect logistics plan or lack of. Now, I must redo all that I worked for, in Miami, here in Marathon. Perhaps, a casual walk will get me the info stuff that will determine what marina and what boat.

This one marina has a similar approach to dock space as the one in Miami that was my target, way back then. Owners, renters, and timeshare owners, must be a Florida thing. It is on the south side of the only road in and out of the Keys, no need to run around the north side to get to an opening to the ocean. While I wait for the proper time to view boaters coming in, I get the sea-scooter and twin tanks from the local dive shop, and some thin, low density styrofoam and glue from the linen shop. At the motel, I glue the styrofoam to all the fixed surfaces of the scooter, reducing echoes from any sonar devices. I gather my gear and place it all in my roller trunk for tonight.

There is not much need for cash where I am going, but the local ATM is hit up for some supper money and a couple of adult beverages to sustain me for the journey tonight. I cannot help but wonder why this ATM machine is blocked by upright pillars to prevent vehicles from approaching and doing business right from the vehicle. I read a posted letter from this bank stating that by year end, all drive up windows must be closed, as ordered by Executive Action of the Federal Government. It seems that the environmentalists have won a major battle with the regime, as if they fought hard, to safeguard the air that we breathe. Idle cars and trucks are wrecking havoc on the ozone layer; air pollution is everywhere and must be curtailed, so they say. So no one has the ability to remain in the car on cold nights, heavy rain, dust storms, or whatever, and must park their vehicle and walk to the ATM or go inside the bank, restaurant, or whatever. Coming back is the foot service to the vehicles from fast food restaurants, taking us back 50, 60, or 70 years when such "conveniences" were an everyday affair. Plenty of work for the minimum wage crowd, I guess.

This just adds on to the environmentalist win side after the "smart electric meters" were required during this POTUS last term. That was well received from the citizens after an intense promotion program by the federal government, again our tax money at work, brainwashing. This current term of POTUS; the electric companies, especially coal fired plants, run brownouts to reduce carbon emissions, not providing notice to the consumers. What a life.

I find a suitable craft, a 24 foot Hurricane, 300 hp engine with a fuel system that 66 gallons of gas will get me there. Sunday night is here, the full moon ended on Friday, so the horizon will be plenty dark, especially with the help of scattered showers. It is time to make my move. 10PM. Move to the sole guard; hope he is not the one I talked to earlier in the day. Nice night, I say, and I asked for the key to boat 13. He demands my ID card, I shove him inside the shack, stun gun him, and he is out. The boat that I want is not 13, but 27. Using his key card to open the lock box, I quickly get to the right panel, thanks to my camera shots. Got the key, grab the trunk, and get to the boat.

I must make sure that all valves are open, the equipment is on, and get away. I cut several boats mooring lines hoping the diversion of drifting boats may delay accounting for the missing boat. Running lights on, engine a go, underway. I make my way out of the docks and into the Atlantic Ocean. Once outside the channel, I go dark, no lights, and watch for other boats. The Coast Guard has been built up in force, something different for this POTUS, who has been downsizing the military for the past six years. More effort to keep citizens from fleeing, not to keep folks out. Straight out southwest for the direct straight shot to Havana. Hit the gas and bounce around some, got to get there in darkness. At 5:05AM, I see the lights of Cuba and work my way just offshore to my drop off point. 23 degrees 12 minutes North Latitude, 82 degrees 21 minutes West Longitude. Just inside a "Particularly Sensitive Sea Area" according to the NOAA Chart 1113A.

I have learned how to do research and better logistics this trip. The idea now is to set this boat on a course eastward using a line on the steering wheel. Dump myself overboard with my gear on and the sea scooter ready to take me inshore. My target is inside the single channel to the docks of this harbor. I know that I must slosh through waters reported to be untreated sewage, industrial waste, and pesticide runoff. The pesticide runoff reminds me of the sad condition of the Chesapeake watershed from farms and the green lawns of many unconcerned residents. And then, there are the sharks. My boat should be on the east side, just inside this channel, to the left. Overboard I go, 3 to 4 miles northeast off of the mouth of the harbor, Havana Bay, and boat away on its own at a slow speed. My GPS float is deployed, under water with my scooter in power. Four miles of travel, 1 hour later, I am in at the entrance, a military installation on each corner.

The entrance itself is not very wide, cruise ships transit this channel without difficulty, 60 feet deep or more, oceanography is not that up to date; I should be able to dive and escape undetected, that is the plan. The tidal range is less than two feet and the current should be minor with the help of this scooter. What I did not plan on is how dark the water is, I know it is night time, no moon, but the living folk above have lights that have no effect in this dense water. My GPS is my guide to 23 degrees 8 minutes 35 seconds North and 82 degrees 20 minutes 5 seconds West of the pier outside corner plus or minus a few feet. Most navy ships, when moored or anchored, leave their sonar on in the passive stage, listening for machinery noises under the surface. Should Cuba have a naval ship in port, a limited navy, one ship in service, last I heard; my scooter will not make noise enough, I hope, to be not picked up by the sonar. Should they activate in the search mode, I am hoping the styrofoam will absorb and scatter the low frequency wave so as not to be detected.

It is now 6:30 and a half hour before sunrise. I see the ready mini sub with one security guard on the floating dock, and then there is another guard at the foot of the pier. Now for the distraction, there must be a dumpster on this pier, every military pier has one. Okay, at the dogleg of the pier, I see a floating dock by it and conveniently, a ladder. As I approach, I say good bye to my scooter, battery nearly dead anyway, and let go to the bottom. Then the 40 pounds of weight, gone too. Quietly onto the floating dock, flippers off, up the ladder with my timer and WP, Willie Pete, aka white phosphorus to produce a fire and intense smoke. Set for seven minutes, to be enough time to swim back to the mini sub float, flippers off, up onto it, then ready to take out the guard. There it goes, a white flash and now smoke, the guard moves to the closest end of the floating dock to get a better look; knowing his orders are to stay with the sub, he will not move from his post, or death will come from his leader. But death arrives sooner. Done. Get my swim gear, keep my GPS stuff for later use, and get into the sub. Now, will all the military and CIA courses on this sub be right? This was the getaway carrier should I get the go to take out Raul. My briefings were to their best knowledge, great.

CHAPTER SIX

SOLO TRAVEL

To the switch panel, fathometer, gyro compass, passive sonar, worry about ballast tanks and buoyancy once underway. One engine to start, valves open that should be, valves closed that should be. Crank over the engine and be heard by the troops, but got to do it now, time a wasting. Loud noise, too loud, they hear. Got to bring in the dock lines and scram, bring in or take in, take it there bring it here, whatever Bobbi Joe, focus, hear the yelling, something, *el barco*, *el barco*, or yea, the boat, the boat. Yes you are right, throttle ahead and turn past the dock to the harbor, *dispara*, *dispara*, I hear, oh, no, shoot, shoot. As I am out of direct sight and shot, I hear *el cable*, *el cable*, at first I thought the curtain, what! Then it became clear, the cable. What cable, I am stretching for a reasonable answer. Then it came to me, during WW1 and WW2, cables were strung across harbors to keep submarines and surface craft out, reducing surprises. That, I thought was an ancient defense, not used nowadays. Realization hit me that Cuba is still in the dark ages in some ways and now I must get past this entrance more quickly.

That part about ballast tanks later, is here. Must dive only below the surface to keep from getting shot at from the corner defenses, yet above the cable, probably being hoisted up from the bottom now. I did not see anything at 25 feet upon entering, but that water was really dark. OK, turn the valves on top of the ballast tanks, lets the air escape and water will come in at the bottom of the tanks through flood gates. This sub is going down and is submerging. The difference between a surface ship and a submarine is the latter can - hopefully - resurface. The positive buoyancy is gone, I am at periscope depth, close the valves, and take a look around. Wow! How did I get past the channel this fast, pure luck, there is a chase boat behind me. I have the depth to go deeper, and say good bye to Cuba.

There is a U.S. Chart # 11013 of Cuba, and Florida Straits, on board, taking me between Florida and the Bahamas, depths in fathoms, old, but useable. Heading for the Straits with my passive sonar at max range, listening for noise of ships or other stuff. My plan is to go half way between northern Cuba and the Keyes of Florida, and then proceed northbound. Soon I need to surface, I am in dire need of fresh air and get this wet suit off of me, it is very hot and confining, both the suit and sub.

The sub is running smooth, some engineer has taken excellent care of the systems, he or she should be proud. Travel northeast, and then creep between the east coast of Florida and The Bahamas. Since it is 8AM, dark at 6PM, at max speed of eleven knots, I can go 100 to 110 miles, close to the west side Cay Sal Banks and shallow water. I know the elite Coast Guard flies fixed wing aircraft and have large watercraft all over the Gulf and ocean looking for druggies or misplaced sailors. I shall clean myself up, then sail alternating on the surface and at a safe depth below the surface to avoid any large tankers or container ships. Less chance of being tracked. The news must be out that a Cuban sub has been hijacked, unless the Cuban Regime is embarrassed, yet the Cuban Resistance Party will get the word out.

Now it is time to reverse the submerging process and return to the surface. First, open the valves for the compressed air to force the water back where it came from, through the flood gates at the bottom of the tanks. Once on surface, I must use the compressor to fill up the compressed air tanks. At periscope depth, full, slow 360 degree look around. The sea surface in quiet for January, I hope the way to the Chesapeake will be the same.

The activities of the Cherry Blossom Season is getting closer, I need enough time for my craft's alterations. All clear, blow out the rest of the water and surface. Switch from batteries to engine. I catch my first breath of fresh, cool, salty air, and can relax for the first time since yesterday afternoon's snooze in preparation for this long day. Cay Sal is a large shoaling area where I will be able to hide behind a shoal, surfaced, and get a restful night sleep, then head out by sunrise or before. Time to eat, what has the chef prepared? The briefings reported that some dry stores are on board, but not known for sure. Some dry stores, canned, or bottled something, maybe? There is coconut water, petit pois (peas), chocolate, yuca (perhaps tapioca) garbanyos (beans). I was going to diet anyway. Wake up tomorrow for 850 miles to Chesapeake Bay Entrance, this will be a long run, with nowhere to rest in peace. And a three day and night continuous run, fatigue will set in, I must rest somehow during this run. Wet suit is off, ate some beans with the water, and now refreshed. My dive wrist unit positioning is confirming the gyro on board. This is a must, especially while underwater. Drop down to about 50 feet of depth, a safe depth, with tremendous depths below me. Set a course of 065 for Double Headed Shot Cays and find a restful place for the night.

5:30PM, time to rise to periscope depth for a look see. This area was not in my briefing, support was to be readily available once outside Cuban territory. My chart is my guide along with my GPS. All clear, rise to the surface. There is a set of binoculars here, useful. There is an old lighthouse on a point of land, I thought the shoals were underwater, but now I see a pleasure boater anchored near the lighthouse site. I will travel a little further north to the backside of the Shot Cays and rest this boat on some very fine white sand. Then there was reef, rock and a little sand. Creeping behind of the shoal and unseen to mariners and poachers, slowly maneuvering to where I could rest the sub aground, yet pull away in the morning, tide willing. That can't be more than two or two and a half feet of rise and fall. Twelve hours from now water will be close to water level now. It is time to refresh with salt water, eat some more beans, and sleep till the alarm hits at 6:00 for a fast getaway and long journey home.

I fully understand that the next 2 or 3 days and nights are going to be nerve racking. Just when I thought the most dangerous part of my plan was the hijacking of a communist sub in their back yard, I am finding out that I may be my own worst enemy, me, myself, and I. With 850 miles of open water, little subsistence, stretching the fuel, and watchdogs on the surface and in the sky, I am almost a cooked goose. This stop over is about 60 miles from the keys and the Gulf Stream is halfway between at its most effectiveness, for a boost as a tail wind. I will hitch a ride underwater between the Bahamas and Florida.

Twelve hours from now, I will be in the mix, the narrowest part of International Waters, with no stopping or any chance of surface cruising. This is a heavy traffic area, stay at least 50 feet below the surface. One terrible thought that crossed my mind is of trawlers and especially their nets, is it dragging season in January, damn if I have a clue. Onward, on the surface for a while, 4 or 5 hours, now, dive to 50 feet, uneventful, so far. A couple of hours under water, and must surface for a while before my descent before 7PM west southwest off of Freeport. Then a north northeast passage to clip the Outer Banks of North Carolina. Stay with the Gulf Stream as long as I can, then turn left, northwest to the Chesapeake. Once 60 miles past the narrow straits, 5 or 6 hours, I go off this chart. I remember that this Gulf Stream continues along the east coast, has a westward arc, until the Outer Banks of North Carolina, Cape Hatteras. At some point I must be on the surface, using my watch GPS to stay at least 30 miles off Hatteras Light.

My GPS receiver is strapped to an exterior bracket, to be used when on the surface and my memory of the mid coast will be my only guides. And now for the fatigue factor. I am able to work 12 hours, sleep 2 hours, and hit it again. But that is not an option when this craft is moving at 14 knots, or 28 miles in those 2 hours. Can't stop, loose time, must be a 20 minute sleep, then up and about, check gauges, autopilot, search the surface, then try sleep another 20. Set the dive watch, passive sonar up to max range and sensitivity, hope for the best. A lot can happen in 4 or 5 miles underwater or surfaces. That westward arc of the Gulf Stream adds at least 20 miles verses the straight shot to the Cape but I would loose that "tailwind" which can be as much as 3 ½ knots at mid center. A quick calculation of the straight shot of 460 miles is 38 plus hours at 12 knots. The arc of the Gulf Stream is 480 miles but a conservative 14 knots would be 34 hours. And consider the warmer water temp of the Gulf Stream will be better for inside living, I will have the Gulf Stream help my progress. That is it.

OK, morning rise, freshen up, and underway to the narrows. One hundred miles on the surface, eat, make sure the equipment is properly set for this long journey. Seven hours later and no close sightings, submerge for a while. Stay down for about one hundred twenty miles or about ten hours and resurface off of Ft. Pierce. Keep a close listen at the passive sonar, passing fish, some dolphins maybe, and a maybe pod of small whales, maybe. The small boats move fast along my scope, but just now, I am picking up something new. The signal is wider than what I have seen so far, and about 6000 yards away, max range for this gear. So I will go to periscope depth for a look see. Three miles away and closing fast is a hugh ship coming at me. Time to go down to about 50 feet, the draft on that monster is probably 40 feet, maybe play it safe, find what 75 feet feels like, my deepest descent so far. The ship is closing over me, directly over and causing some turbulence for this boat, kicking us around a little. Shake, shake, shake it off, sing it, Taylor Swift, shake it off. The depth finder has me up and down, not staying at 75, hitting 60 then 80 feet, but now the turbulence is diminishing, oh, so slowly. On the sonar, I see the ship is heading away from me in the same relative direction it came in on, the starboard bow aspect. Wait a second, check the autopilot, it is off, tripped off in the turbulence, and the sub is heading back to where we came from. That last mix turned us around, now to get back on an even keel and direction, set the pilot one more time. Surface for some fresh air ASAP.

At 2330, should be out of the narrows, periscope depth, all clear, up we go. End of day two underway in a mini-sub. Havana to Ft. Pierce. On the surface all night long, no lights, sleep in cat naps, hope for the best. Ocean is still calm, good to have. Around 0700, descend for a while and once past St. Augustine, sixty miles later, the Gulf Stream makes a slight turn NNE. Surface for a while. Off of Georgia, a right turn NE, at about 31 North Latitude, and the Gulf Stream is slowing down to about a knot and a half. At 2100, my sonar is making a pinging noise, something I have not initiated, mine is not a search sonar, just a listening device, so what's up out there?

I look around and no navy vessels in sight. On the surface, that is. Somewhere in the St. Marys Entrance is the navy's trident submarine base, Kings Bay, Georgia, thanks to the peanut farmer, Jimmie Carter, POTUS # 39. Have I just crossed the pathway that these subs use in and out of port, what terrible luck?

The good luck is that my profile is small, like a whale, now what do whales do? I should have paid more attention to that pod yesterday and took some lessons. So make like a whale, dive to 20 feet, rise up, dive slightly less, rise up, dive deeper, and rise up, see what happens. Do not be consistent, do not do the same maneuvering twice, whales don't. An hour later, still the pinging. A tanker is on my starboard, heading NE toward Georgia, maybe Savannah, remember that turbulence yesterday! Use this ship to our advantage, cross under, and stay with it close to the hull, then peel off. But how close?

How accurate is this sonar anyway, a hundred foot error could be disastrous. And I can only go so far off of the Gulf Stream westward keeping in mind the Outer banks of North Carolina jet eastward in that US curve. This is a must do to get rid of the tracking sub. Get behind the ship, go to periscope depth and close in safely, that will work. The ships range is decreasing on my starboard side, shake, shake, wait, shake, wait, let it pass, rise up. Shake, rattle and roll. In the turbulence, astern of the ship, shake some more, steering is hard, staying level is difficult, and away, the ship rips away from me. Maybe eight knots relative speed away. Ok, now turn NE with the current and hope to be on the other side of this noise from the sub, which is my guess. What a way to end day three, around 31-30 North Latitude.

Somewhere around 0630 and off of Georgetown, South Carolina, made it past Charleston offshore with no incident. No subs this time. Heading NE toward Cape Fear, North Carolina, Cape Lookout, then Cape Hatteras, 140 miles ahead, eta 1730. Dive to 50 feet, this is getting old, boring, got to fight fatigue. Once at Hatteras, make the turn to the NW toward the Chesapeake eta there 0330. And the end of day three or is it day four, no food, some water, dear me, what have I gotten into? The AM radio on here was not receiving anything but stations that jump at night, not good reception. Today, however, so close to shore - that is a relative term - I received a North Carolina station. News reports catching me up on the POTUS and her friends. What are they doing now? Last year, shut down some Air Force squadrons, and removed the Chief of the Joint Chiefs of Staff, mighty bold move. Now it seems, that hostile enemy that was in my sights by the way, has threatened to use dirty bombs in major US cities, unless we pull all forces out of Europe and Africa, he said ALL.

Maybe that is why so much downsizing, blackmail, deadly threats. The US of A does not back down, up to POTUS 46 and 47, that is. She wanted this crisis, do not let a good crisis go to waste, but she did not expect to be placed in check. She is talking about delaying all federal elections next year for two years, ripping away Amendments 15 and 19 to the Constitution, giving her more dictatorship time, I bet. In our democracy, the ability to vote for our representatives is foremost in our rights of citizenship.

If we have a terrible politician, we wait till next election and hopefully vote that dumb ass out and replace her or him with another dumb ass. But, by this Executive Order she is so wrong. Just when I was enjoying this luxury cruise, she is back in my life.

And, out of fuel, OH CRAPOLA. The fuel cell -powered system is good for 15 days underwater, just recharged last time I surfaced. How did it charge, never gave it much thought, but I do need to know and now, without the main fuel supply. But that crisis may be behind me. After I made the turn to the Chesapeake, 1330 hours, loosing the depth of water, what was several hundred feet deep, is now a hundred. I need some depth for hiding as I approach the entrance in pure daylight. Now to find that depth. Can't find any more than 50 feet, yikes, what about a big ship over my head, no clearance at all. Must keep vigilant, stay to the edge of the channel, or outside of it with satisfactory depth. Slowed my speed to a creep. In and out turns in the Chesapeake for 65 miles till I turn left for the Potomac River, Thank God.

Dark has come as I turn up the Potomac River, perfect. Not as much commercial traffic of any great depth. Not much more distance to go, and home is there. Twenty two or twenty three miles. Guided by periscope. Once I leave the channel, I must be as low in the water that depth allows so as not to be seen. I recognize the two flashing yellow breakwater lights marking Piney Point, it will not be long now, be cautious of your surroundings, on the water and below, for depth. Don't want to run aground now, so close. Seventeen feet, sixteen feet, ten feet, draft 3 feet, doing ok so far. I placed colored reflector tape on the water side of the boathouse, but how to see it without a light hitting it, shit. I need a flash light, did not see such a thing on board. Got to stop engine, search one out. Even so, I will be seen, another shit. What am I doing, the GPS on my wrist is for what, look at it dummy. You placed the precise positioning data in it before ya left a long time ago, it seems; use it now. That's better, inch forward, nine feet, seven feet, there is home, the boathouse I mean. Hooray. Grab the remote I left on the down river outside piling and open the door.

Just inside, get off, feet on firm ground, well, I mean the deck; raise the small boat and maneuver the sub by its mooring line into its sling. Open the submerge tank valve to gently sink the sub in the cradle, close the hatch, leaving the small boat afloat. End of day four. Eat, drink, and be happy, happy, and happy. Go to bed.

CHAPTER SEVEN

THE WEAPONRY

My contacts in the Middle East are telling me that this POTUS is so far off base of the perceived threat that was available for the kill, if only allowed. Someone is going to pull the trigger and chance a Court Martial to save this Country, not from Omar Abu Haggina, but from this female POTUS. End the dire threat, of him, Omar, or her, POTUS, I wonder. But this is not the only error of POTUS thinking; loosing the itemized deduction only bothered some, the working class; delaying general elections two years only bother some people that follow politics; but initiating Martial Law?

WOW! That takes everyone in. Defined as: **control by armed forces:** the control and policing of a civilian population by military forces and according to military rules, imposed, e.g. in wartime or when the civilian government no longer functions. Maybe my term is wrong, since the government is in full control, by threats of use of force by the police departments and the military. Amendment 4 to the Constitution be damned, unreasonable searches and seizures are occurring. Remember the MRAP, the Mine Resistant Ambush Protected Vehicles seen at various police stations? This country as a whole has never seen curfew hours and passes needed to go to work or home, very stressful. Amendment One of the Constitution has just been amended by Executive Action, no right to peaceably assemble, and no right to petition the government. My, have we been sold a bad, bad piece of goods in this girl or girls, that is.

Time is a wasting, now for the surface to surface missile and the material for the rail mounted launcher. There will be some alterations of the launcher to make it adaptable on the sub for a direct mount. And to also refuel the sub, get some diesel. Along the shoreline of Virginia, Dahlgren specifically, is a naval support facility that is used for developing and testing of new munitions, a proving ground complete with two separate runways. This facility is about 30 miles upriver and on the opposite side. The Warfare Center, my target, is at 38 Degrees, 19 Minutes, 10.32 Seconds North 77 Degrees, 01 Minutes, 52.11 Seconds West. Exact position is needed for my GPS dive watch and maneuvering the mini sub to where I can swim to shore. The round trip will be a good exercise for my final run up to DC at Cherry Bloom time.

This navy unit has been developing a GPS guided missile small enough for the mini sub to carry and fire. The DAGR, Direct Attack Guided Rocket is already in service, but the navy has a new use and wants to set a geographical position into the rocket, so no direct laser is needed, just set position, and send it on its way. It carries a ten pound high explosive warhead with a super-quick fuse to explode immediately upon impact. Damage radius is around 10 yards with a lethal radius 50 yards from metal fragments, enough to do the job. Accuracy is within a yard. My kind of War on this Woman.

Dahlgren's Base Guide has a lot of beneficial info from facilities to recreation. All for the reading on the internet. Then a good view from overhead with Google Earth and local charts on line. Makes for a good risk assessment to get in, get the goods, and get out. I will use the small boat left behind by the kind landlord to launch my drone and evaluate the security measures that must be all around this installation. There are two marked channels, 8 feet deep at low water entering or approaching the base. Upon entering the waterway intersection of the Potomac and Upper Machodoc Creek; I notice a fix structure, a light on a piling where I will be able to tie up the sub and gently sink it next to the structure without flooding me out. And a half mile swim to the landing site. The 35 pound rocket and the extra 5 pound GPS brain will be no problem to carry back to the sub, and off we go. That is the plan.

Thirty miles did not seem so long a trip as compared to the run from Havana to Piney Point, and my stomach is happy, once again. The drone is showing high frequency active infrared detectors mounted on poles at knee height all around the perimeter. Knowing that there are dual beams that both must be interrupted for an alarm to be noticed, I have the ability to bend the IR by mirrors that will not be noticed. I certainly cannot go over the beams with 40 pounds of contraband on my shoulder. The only way this alteration would be seen is by a guard walking the line, and that is an unknown. Security cameras need to be watched for effectiveness and no gaps between cameras for 100 percent coverage. Their error is along sides of the building, cameras facing outward do not watch the walls where I make my advance. Friday nights, things slack off and my guess is that I will have the time needed for my quick round trip to the lab. The lab itself has key pad security and that was easily seen as one unsuspecting critter entered his "private" number at the door. The drone is so quiet, that a mosquito makes more of a racket, as it hovered over the back of his head. Got it. Back to the boathouse.

CHAPTER EIGHT

GET THE GOODS

Once dark came around, I took the mini-sub out of Piney Point, upriver along the western edge of the channel, staying around the twenty foot curve, out of the way of passing boaters and low enough to be out of sight, hopefully. The batteries are fully charged, engine running quietly so as not to disturb the flocks of birds hanging around the water's edge. No need to attract attention. The channel swings to the left - uh port - but I stay along the right curve out of notice. Then it gets a little hairy, the curve is jagged with shoals right in the middle of the river, how nice. I must watch for the buoys marking the deepest channel as I move over to the west side of the river. My wrist GPS is no use when the depth of water is concerned, fathometer and aids to navigation have to be the safest way. About a mile from Dalgren is a marked channel with a 7 foot depth where I can follow it to the mooring. This three foot draft is amazing for navigating out of the river, then to the piling marked number 5, where I shall leave the sub temporally. The depth of water is six feet, so I can open the ballast tank valves, lay the sub gently on the bottom with top side above the water surface with room to spare for opening the hatch. Wetsuit has been on; add the flippers, mask, and snorkel, and mirror configuration is in my booty bag.

One half mile swim, I am ashore. Switch gear in the bag, don my IF lens glasses, divergent gear ready, and crawl up the shore line to the brush. Once to the rocks, there are plenty, the edge closest to the buildings, I have located the IR detectors, and my setup is in place. Across the grass, to the seawall, to the corner of the building, nice convenience to have the lab close to the test area, thanks. Back to the wall, sidestepping to the right door with the key pad, and I am in. Stop immediately inside and look around. There was no way of knowing if IR detectors are on the inside, look with my glasses, hope this door is not in its sight.

This secure facility has all the storage units locked and labeled, again, nice, thanks. Military protocol of course. I find the storage locker marked "armed prototype" and with a bent paper clip, open the lock. Got it, a complete DAGR. Next locker to look for is the spare GPS's modified for the new test subjects. Still look around for IR detectors. Got that locker labeled too, my good fortune. Open up sesame, boxes labeled tested, ready for flight, get one and get gone. Make sure both locks are in place and locked, not noticeable till Monday. Then all hell will break loose here. Out the door, return same way to the seawall, pass under my mirrors, grab them quickly, over the rocks, thru the bushes, and to the booty bag.

Move it, move it, quickly, remove swim gear, pack the booty, don gear, swim back to sub. There it is, still, was I expecting something else? Off with the gear, open the hatch, lower the gear, release the mooring line, rid some of the ballast water, and head downstream. Stay on the west side until past the center shoals, and then make the crossing to the 20 curve once more. No boats out tonight, everyone enjoying TGIF day. Four hours to get there, short time ashore, four hours run back home, and daylight is approaching, so is the boathouse. Mission accomplished, done, rest time.

CHAPTER NINE

OMAR ABU HAGGINA IS DEAD

What this POTUS Administration did not have the courage or desire to do; Israel did with one hot missile up Omar's ass and exploding him all over his holy land. One time, Israel was the main friend of the US in the Middle East until the most previous POTUS apologized to our enemies, Israel's enemies, for our aggressions. Never to back down or weaken their nation's security, Israel decidedly took action that the US had a reputation for doing, years ago, but no more. This action must be a slap in the face of our holiness and her administration. Now we can go back to normalcy. Gone should be the martial law, the curfews, the passes for going to another state, and most importantly, returning to the scheduled general elections, yea!. The right to bear arms, the Second Amendment, shall become honored again.

What are POTUS and VPOTUS doing on TV? This is impossible; situation is still dangerous for the country even with Omar dead? We need to gather around the Administration, support strategies that will keep us safe. CRAP! That is a bunch of CRAP! The citizens will not take this anymore, they have protested the curfews, protested the martial law, fed up with the brown outs; this is a remembrance of the civil rights marches in the 60's.

The majority leaders of the House and Senate have been arrested for possible treason charges, ludicrous. What she has just done is to eliminate the opposing party from the succession order: first, of course, the VPOTUS, then the Speaker of the House (in custody), President Pro Tempore of the Senate - I guess the Majority Leader was also Pro whatever (in custody), then the Cabinet Members, her appointees; of course, eliminating all opposition in the succession list. The crown is hers and hers, together.

A coup d'état of sorts, without a shot fired. Well, not so fast, there are and were the tear gas firings to dispel all of the demonstrators all over the land in protests. My guess is there will be deaths as the native uprising gets to the critical mass level, shortly. So onward with the plan. This is so against my principles, never thought that I would go thru with it, just gave me a challenge. Now I soon will be the traitor to the Presidency and to this Country. I shall disappear from here, not knowing if the government figured the "hit" out. Hopefully, not.

I must remove the gyro, auto pilot, and disconnect some other electrical components before I spot weld the brackets to the sub's forward topside hull. Then attach the rocket launcher so it will last for just one shot. Once that is done, reconnect the electrics. Now program the GPS in the missile to climb up and over the tallest building, stay just above, then set the position 38 degrees 55 minutes 16.59 seconds north, 77 degrees 3 minutes 49.17 seconds west at an elevation of 400 above sea level. Tallest building in direct path is less than 230 feet; just prior to launch, I must adjust the barometer setting to the current pressure so the device can accurately know the heights of flying.

How advanced this GPS is in knowing advance and transfer while in flight to compensate ahead so as to be right above the set position, then head directly down, straight down. While waiting for high noon at the bridge, set the laptop to drive the auto pilot to the points down river to the Chesapeake, then to the ocean and seaward, where it will explode, if not earlier.

Saturday evening is near, I must ready, set, and go upstream now. The run to Dalgren helped me adjust to shallow water navigation and to be of utmost attention at every second of this round trip. Going upstream will be so dangerous, not knowing what underwater devices are in place to catch critters like me. Sonar buoys on the surface or set on the bottom, other unknowns that I do not know about. It is so difficult not to know what I do not know.

Dalgren is on my port, buoys do a good, good job of marking where the channel is. I am on the edge at periscope depth, 20 feet of water, going well. A place called Kettle Bottom Shoals has many bumps and hills to wiggle around, 14 feet, then drops to 70 and 80 feet, quite something. Could this be where sound devices are located, along the pilings? Got to do it, keep going. There is a sharp turn to the southwest, something like a snake slithering along the ground, nice metaphor. It is amazing how the west side of the channel is 2 and 4 feet deep, yet the east side can be 65 to 70 feet deep.

From Piney Point to launch site is 90 miles of curves, hills from the bottom, bridges, and that unknown underwater detection equipment. I will go max speed, slow when needed, got to be in place before sunrise. This run can take around 8 to 10 hours, depending. Wow, I should not have been be so surprised at this sharp left turn to the southwest after heading northerly so far. At this turn, I am loosing some depth too, less than 30 feet. Stick with the edge of the channel; bottom comes up fast on the right, shoals on the left, watch for surface traffic. Channel narrows as it swings to the north northwest, then north.

Now, across from Quantico Marine Base. I have been there, after my Parris Island visit, boot camp; I was sent directly to Quantico for more marksmanship training. This is troubling, there is a sting of yellow, green, and red lights across the entire channel; is that a detection device system, not good, if so. As I approach, the lights display warnings of overhead power lines held up by fixed structures, that could be real, but Homeland Security or the Coast Guard may have use for the bases as well.

Troubling. There is a slight upstream current, so shut the engine down, the fath, and passive sonar, drift through it. Wait until far distant or endanger of running aground before lighting off the stuff again. The return may not be so cautious; time will be of the essence. Ok, folks, start your engine, the markers display a narrow channel that I must transit to an opening channel bending eastward, then northerly. Eastward again. I have good depth again, and this is fun, for just a moment.

Now approaching Fort Washington on the starboard - the right - side, then Alexandria on the left, next. Who-ha! The channel really narrows now. I am at my first bridge, the Woodrow Wilson Bridge. I am not going into the cleared opening; will edge around to where I can have a few feet under, still stay hidden from sight. Passing clear, back to the marked channel, across from The Ronald Reagan Airport, sir, I hope you are resting in peace; you would not want to see your Country today. At Mount Rushmore; Washington, Jefferson, and Lincoln have turned their heads in disbelief, and Theodore Roosevelt is contemplating what in the world is happening.

Citizens being killed for exercising their First Amendment Rights. This is where I must leave the marked primary channel and turn left for the old 14th Street Bridge, my hideaway till noontime. The channel is on the west side, I will rest on the east side in 7 feet of water right next to an abutment. At this point, the target is 3.5 miles straight shot, near the max distance for this DAGR.

CHAPTER TEN

THE DEATH BLOW

My wrist alarm goes off at 1100, rested easily once alongside and valves opened to sit on the bottom for a couple of hours. The VPOTUS hosts a Cheery Blossom Adult Picnic for the POTUS, her Cabinet, and her party's leaders of the House and Senate. Unlike the State of the Union Report by the POTUS, no Cabinet Member stays absent. Her ideology friends gather to brag about last year's success and to make strategies for the current year. The Majority Leaders in the House and Senate remain in house arrest.

The police, local, state, and federal have clamped down on all protests, stopping anything as it starts, before a gathering gets up any steam. The liberal media has always wanted to make changes in this country as they see it, now with this Administration; they finally have their chance with the enormous support of POTUS and VPOTUS. Back scratching at the highest possible level.

The atmospheric pressure is 29.92 millibars, so I set the GPS on the rocket to maintain the tightest accuracy during flight. I am listening to the AM radio, WFED 1500 on your dial, covers federal government news. Since it is Sunday, and no government stories, they cover the picnic, from outside the fence and gates. I have got to have my 2 tasks ready to go, first, place the rocket in the launcher; meaning rise up to water's edge, high enough not to drown, yet low enough not to be seen. Launch and the next task is to get out of Dodge City.

Looking around with the periscope, I see the militia at the foot of the bridge, guards at the center of the bridge, so much for this martial law. The radio station reports all hands on deck, now is the time, rise up slowly, only need to surface to the level where the rocket launcher is above the water.

Will see how observant the guards are, this will only take a few seconds, then bam. The noise is certainly going to cause my position to be compromised, be ready to close hatch and open valves, turn sub around, and beat feet. If I am sighted, there will be numerous aerial surveillance looking for me.

FIRE the rocket. Damn, the noise is louder than I ever imagined, shit. A cloud or streak forms from the rocket; close the hatch, dive, dive, yare, right, in seven feet of water. I do not know what happened to the rocket, my head is on the periscope, navigating away from the bridge staying as deep as the bottom will allow, and hoping no hill is ahead. I head back to the main channel south of Potomac Park. Now I will stay in the marked channels as long as I can at the most speed that I can do. Was I seen?

The twists and turns slow me down, unlike the GPS on the rocket; I have nothing to help me with this sub's advance and transfer, no one but me. On the inbound route, I did not hear any pinging underwater, a source of possible detecting devices, should I hear that now, that will be sonar buoys dropped from the air or dumped from a surface vessel, looking for a sub. It is going to be a long 90 mile return to safety. I am sure Quantico, Dalgren, and other military installations have gone to DEFCO ONE, the highest level of readiness and will have surface craft covering the river. I am still cruising along, no pinging, surface craft are moving around but the waters deepen and I am confident of following my track in reverse of my earlier route.

The chain of command has shifted, if the rocket was successful. The Leaders of the House and Senate should be released, and become leaders again, as if they lost that attribute, only restricted for a period of time. Now the country should have a new POTUS, the Leader of the House of Representatives. Then, he will nominate a VPOTUS once the dust settles. If so, the martial law will soon be lifted, as well as curfews, and restrictions of movement. This will not happen right away, they must find the culprit that did the disastrous, dirty deed.

CHAPTER ELEVEN

THE ESCAPE

B ack at the boathouse, must make a fast turnaround of the sub, connect the laptop with the GPS float line, and to the auto pilot. The floating device will be trailing the sub, the cable through the hatch, a water tight seal maybe or maybe not. The laptop receives the data where it is at, has preprogrammed geographical points where it will tell the auto pilot directions downstream, then to the ocean. I have a best guess of how much to open the ballast valves to keep the sub underwater at a safe depth so as not to run aground, yet, not to be spotted.

It is a straight shot, 22 miles to the Chesapeake River, then a right 62 miles to the Bay Bridge. This is where the GPS really needs to tell the right positions, to get through without hitting a bridge structure. Once that is passed, a left to the ocean, east for 200 miles. Connect WP to the ballast valves with an electric donator via the batteries and laptop, so it will blow at 2000 fathoms of water depth. Another WP attached to inside the hatch, triggered to blow if hatch is opened. I am so nice, a laminated warning on the outside of the hatch, good girl. This will take a bit of coordination, sub in sling, raring to go, valves open, GPS float deployed. Set your craft in motion, good bye.

This is Monday; my escape will not be so easy. I will take my landlord's car to Richmond Virginia International Airport where I will meet up with my tour group for our adventure to the Marshall Islands, Pacific Atoll, via Honolulu. There certainly will be some flight delays because of the racket in DC, but not too long. The landlord pointed out the much easier access to this airport in times of crisis or a normal routine; he will pick up his car from the long term lot next month. That works for me. Return the boat house slings to normal by releasing the under carry stuff. Just drop to the water bottom keeping his boat at the ready. Check cautiously for any, any items reflecting back at the tenant. Clean up the house, make secure, and leave a nice note to keep the deposit. Enjoyed the stay.

Since I have his car, I must remain in the name of his tenant for verification, but at the airport I will be my own, back to Bobbi Joe going on a vacation. Oh, the island is so nice, I want to stay, tour group return without me kind of yak, yak.

"Bobbi Joe, Bobbi Joe, wake up we are here, wake up sleepy head." What am I hearing? "Wake up." "Girl, you crashed before we took off from Jeddah, you tired or something?" Where am I, I asked? San Diego was the reply. Huh? "OK, Bobbi, eighteen hours straight sleep on this non-stop from Jeddah International Airport to San Diego, are you kidding me? You slept that long, even with the in-air refueling."

So I ask, what are we doing in San Diego, Colonel? "Gunnery Sergeant, your new orders are for you to take over the armory at Beale Air Force Base, don't you remember your orders, Sarg?" I am coming around, what happened in SA? He said our mission was complete, 100 percent. Well okay, I am good with that, but why are you calling me Gunnery Sergeant, I am an E-6, a Staff Sargent, sir? "Bobbi, you had plenty of sleep, head is still with cobwebs, your promotion came just before we left SA, when our mission was completed." I just had to ask, is the POTUS the same as when we left the states last year, regretting the question after it was asked?

"Yes, same o, same o, stuff, routine stuff, why do ya ask?" OH NOTHING, SIR, thanks.

END